Sebastian Meschenmoser was born in Frankfurt, Germany, in 1980. He studied
fine arts in Mainz, Germany. His illustrations were chosen from more than 2,700 entries
and presented at the Children's Book Fair in Bologna in recognition of him being one
of the most innovative new illustrators. As an accomplished artist with several exhibitions
to his name, Sebastian Meschenmoser is among Germany's most successful and admired
young illustrators for children.

First published in the United States, Great Britain, Canada, Australia, and New Zealand in 2016
by NorthSouth Books Inc., an imprint of Nord-Süd Verlag AG, CH-8005 Zürich, Switzerland.
Distributed in the United States by NorthSouth Books Inc., New York 10016.
Library of Congress Cataloging-in-Publication Data is available.

ISBN: 978-0-7358-4261-8
Printed in China by Leo Paper Products Ltd., Heshan, Guangdong, May 2016.
1 3 5 7 9 • 10 8 6 4 2
www.northsouth.com

MIX
Paper from
responsible sources
FSC® C020056

Pug Man's 3 Wishes

Text and illustrations by Sebastian Meschenmoser

North
South

One morning Pug Man woke up and the day was already half over.

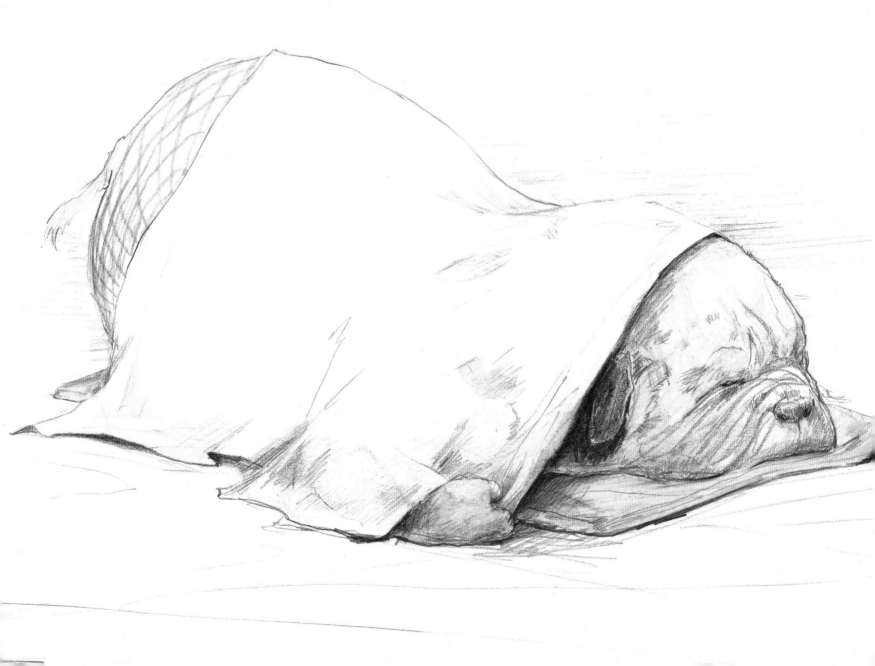

"Is it worth getting up at all just for half a day?" he wondered.

No milk in the fridge . . .

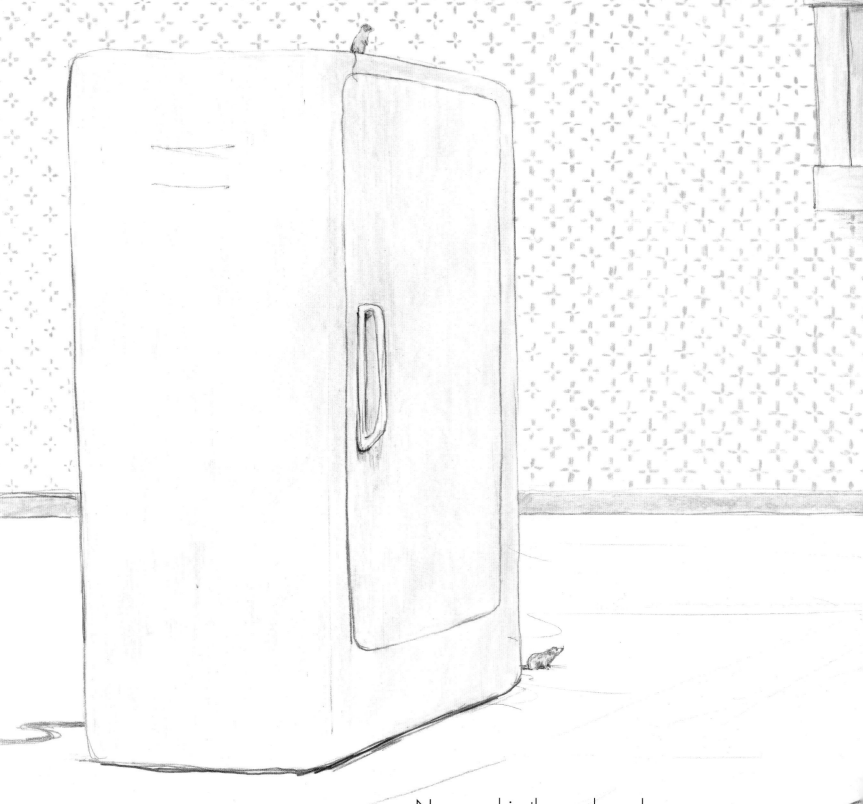

No cereal in the cupboard . . .

No coffee in the cup . . .

"I wonder if the newspaper has come."

It was a bad day for Pug Man.
Wet newspaper, no breakfast, and no coffee . . .

It was so bad that Pug Man wished he'd stayed in bed for the other half.

POP!

Suddenly a fairy appeared.

The fairy said:

"Raspberry drops and creamy cake,
Chocolate of every type and make,

"Purple kitten, piglet, pony,
So you needn't feel so lonely.

POP!

"Castle, car, swimming pool,
You've got three wishes—that's the rule.

"Pick three things you'd like to come true,
while I'm sitting here with you."

Isn't the little fairy great?

"Number 1"

"Number 2"

"Number 3"

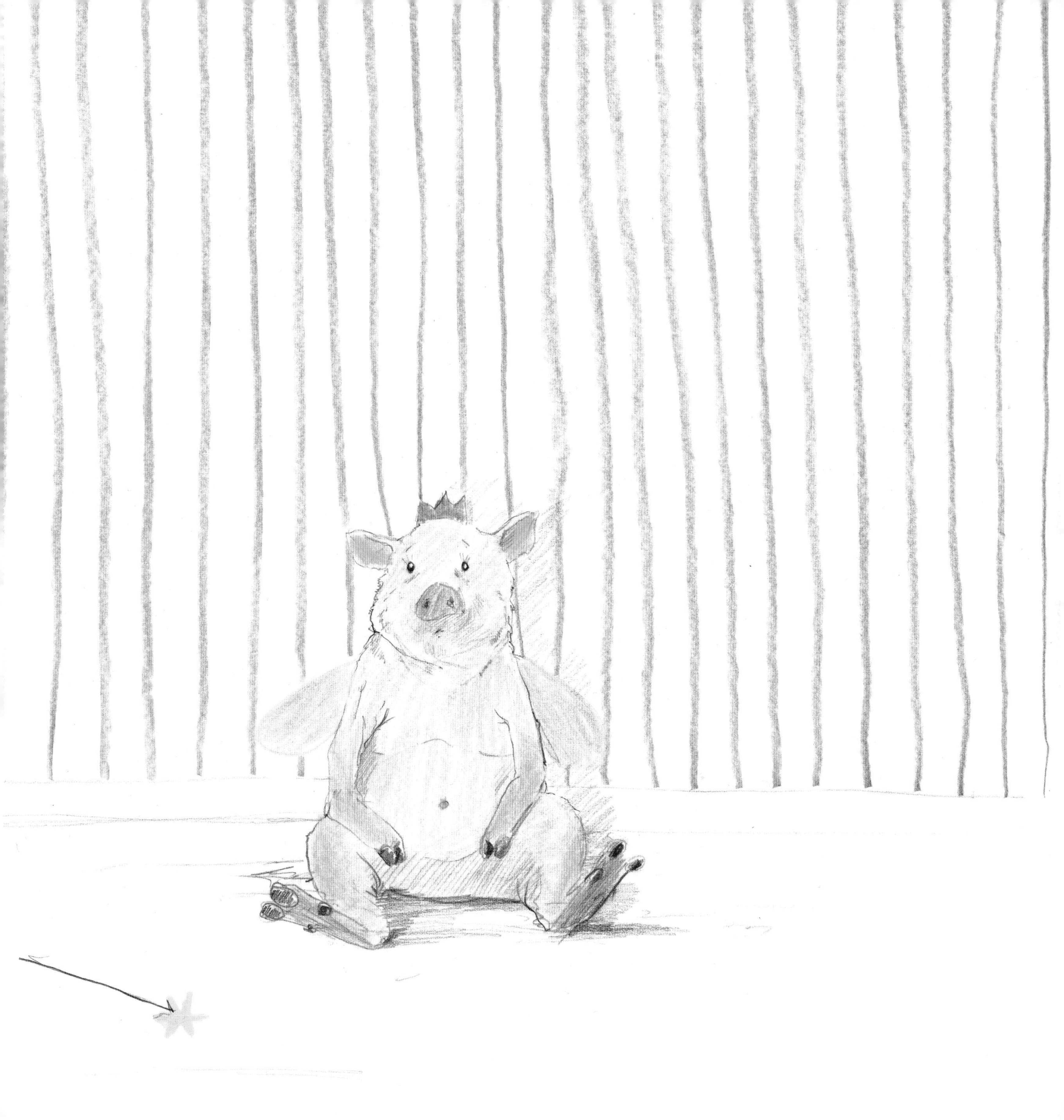

And so Pug Man and Princess Piglet lived happily ever after for the rest of their days (some half and some whole).